Straight to the POLE

First published in the United States of America
in 2003 by Walker Publishing Company, Inc.

Published simultaneously in Canada by Fitzhenry and
Whiteside, Markham, Ontario L3R 4T8

For information about permission to reproduce selections from this book,
write to Permissions, Walker & Company, 435 Hudson Street, New York,
New York 10014

Library of Congress Cataloging-in-Publication Data

O'Malley, Kevin, 1961-
   Straight to the Pole / Kevin O'Malley.— [1st U.S. ed.]
      p. cm.
      Summary: A boy who is struggling through snow to get to
   school is about to give up but then hears some good news from
   his friends.
   ISBN 0-8027-8866-1 (HC) -– ISBN 0-8027-8868-8 (RE)
      [1. Snow—Fiction.] I. Title

PZ7.O526St 2003
[E]—dc21   2002192408

The artist used watercolors on 240-pound watercolor paper
to create the illustrations for this book. Line work was created
with a quill pen and blended Higgins inks.

Book design by Nicole Gastonguay

Visit Walker & Company's Web site at www.walkerbooks.com

Printed in Hong Kong
10 9 8 7 6 5 4 3

For EMILY

Straight to the POLE

Kevin O'Malley

Walker & Company

New York

Frozen and alone.

Pressing on
through the snow.

Pushing
through
the wind.

Over hills

and mountains.

SLIDING.

Bone-chilling wind
biting my cheeks.

must go on.

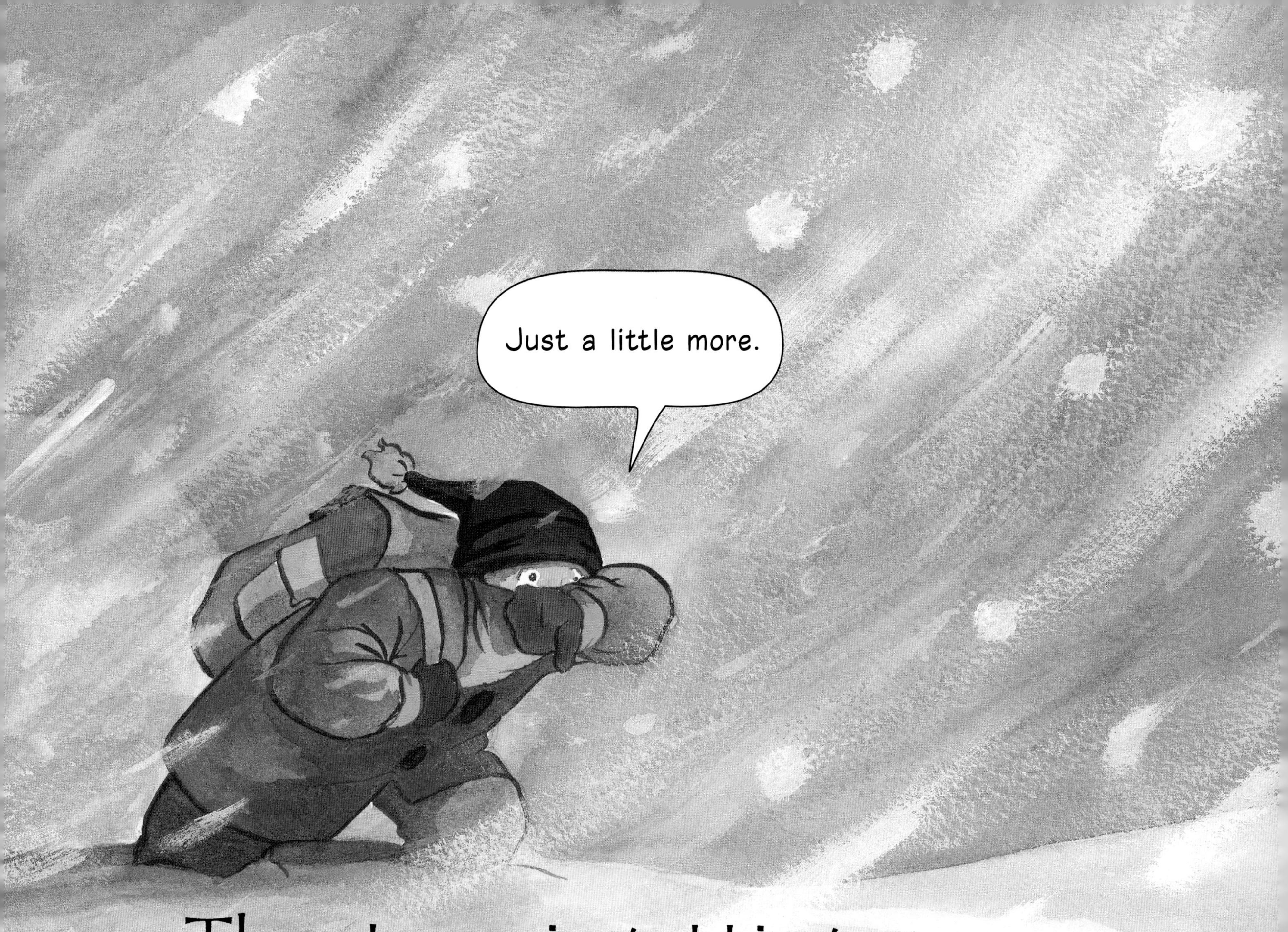

The storm is getting worse.

The ice and snow have
filled up my boots.

CAN'T . . . GO . . .

Oh no . . .

A WOLF!

Lost and alone. . .

WON'T SOMEBODY

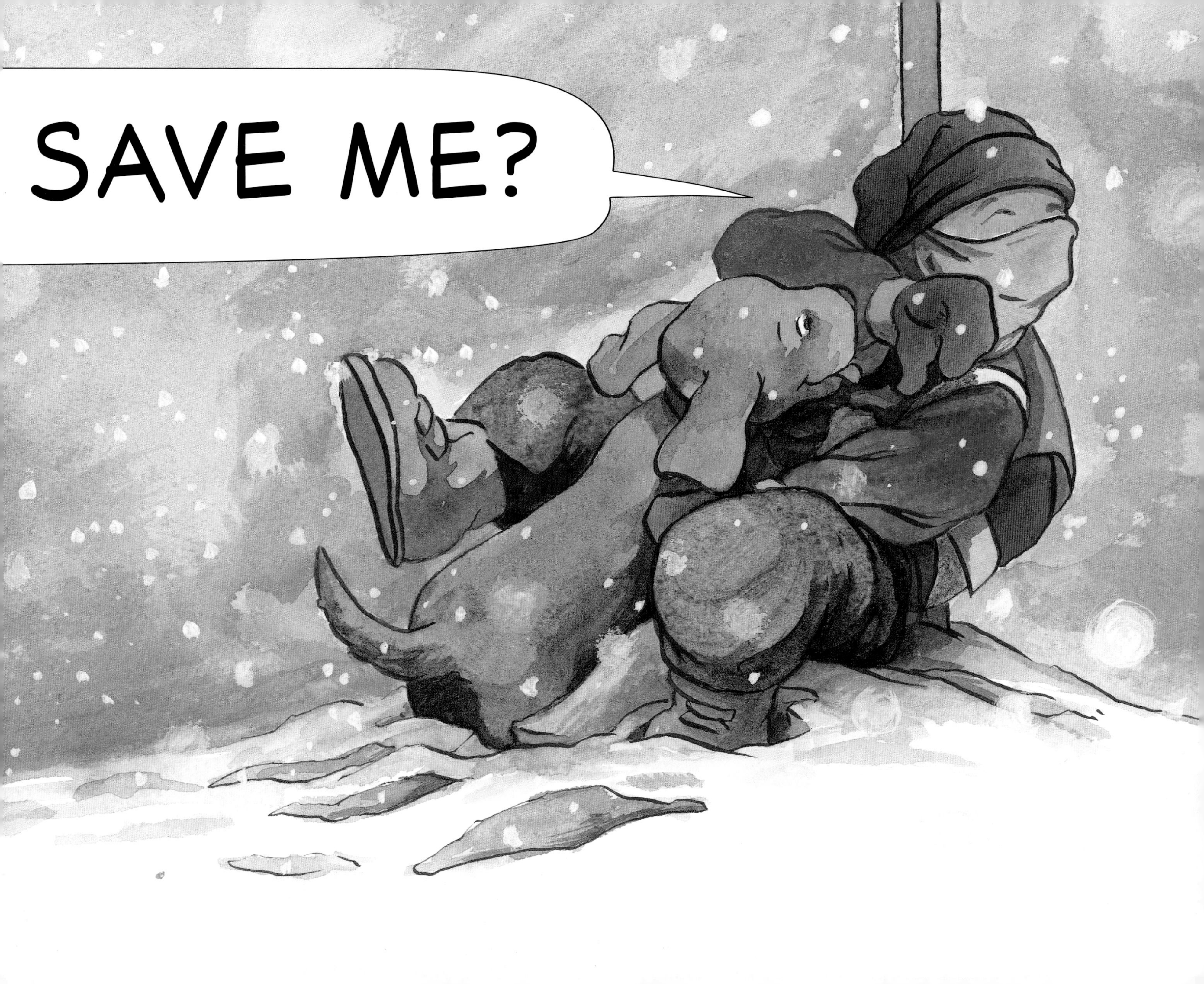
SAVE ME?

But wait,

in the distance,

A RESCUE.

My friends

tell me that
school has been

closed for the day!

HOORAY!